NOTE TO PARENTS

Based on the beloved Walt Disney motion picture *101 Dalmatians*, this book focuses on what happens after Cruella De Vil steals the Dalmatian puppies from Pongo and Perdita. As the parents begin their long and difficult search they realize that cooperation is the key to rescuing their puppies.

Pongo and Perdita use the dog-to-dog relay system known as the Twilight Bark to spread the word about the kidnapping. From London to the countryside, dogs cooperate by barking the message to their nearest neighbors. Finally the bark reaches the Colonel, an old sheepdog who discovers the puppies being held prisoner in the De Vil mansion. The Colonel relays the information back to London, and Pongo and Perdita set out to rescue their puppies. With all the puppies working together, and the cooperation of some friends along the way, the 101 Dalmatians escape from Cruella and return safely to their home.

This book recounts memorable episodes from the movie that will help children learn an important lesson about the value of cooperation. For the complete story of **Walt Disney's *101 Dalmatians***, look for these other Golden Books:

Walt Disney's 101 DALMATIANS

Escape from Danger

A BOOK ABOUT COOPERATION

Adapted by Justine Korman / Illustrated by Bill Langley and Ron Dias

A GOLDEN BOOK • NEW YORK
Western Publishing Company, Inc., Racine, Wisconsin 53404

Once there was an evil woman named Cruella De Vil who loved nothing but fur coats and fast cars. One day she visited her old school chum Anita and Anita's husband, Roger.

"Hello, darlings!" Cruella exclaimed, breezing into the house, wearing a new fur coat.

Roger and Anita's Dalmatian dogs, Pongo and Perdita, growled in the corner, guarding their puppies. They hated Cruella De Vil.

"What have we here?" Cruella cooed when she saw the fifteen puppies. "What beautiful coats they have!" she said, stroking their soft spotted fur. A cruel light sparkled in her eyes.

"Name your price!" Cruella declared. "I must have all
fifteen."

Pongo growled and Roger shook his head.

"I'm sorry, Cruella," Anita explained, "but it would break
Perdita's heart if we sold even one."

With a swirl of her long fur coat Cruella stormed out of the house.

"What I can't buy I'll steal!" she vowed as she revved up her roadster and sped away on screeching tires.

Then one wintry night, while Pongo and Perdita were out walking with Roger and Anita, Cruella sent her thugs to snatch the puppies from their cozy wicker bed.

Pongo and Perdita were horrified to discover that their puppies were gone.

"It's that evil woman Cruella De Vil," Perdita said, sobbing. "She has stolen our puppies! Oh, Pongo, do you think we'll ever find them?"

"Not by ourselves," Pongo said. "But with help we might get our puppies back."

While on their walk the next night, Pongo barked as loudly as he could.

"Shhh!" Roger said. "You'll wake all of London."

But that was exactly what Pongo wanted to do.

"Calling all dogs," he barked. "Urgently need your help!"

Pongo waited for someone to answer his barks, but it was a very cold night and most dogs were inside. Then Perdita joined her bark to Pongo's, and at last they heard a reply.

"Message received. Most sorry about your puppies. Will do all I can to help spread the word," howled a Great Dane on Hampstead Heath.

The tale of the fifteen kidnapped Dalmatian puppies was carried on the dog-to-dog relay system known as The Twilight Bark. From hound to poodle, poodle to shepherd, shepherd to mutt, the story spread all over London.

The Twilight Bark even reached a quiet farm in Sussex where an old sheepdog known as the Colonel slept.

"Alert, alert!" shouted Sergeant Tibs, a cat who lived on the farm. "Vital message coming in from London over The Twilight Bark."

The Colonel sprang to attention. "What's going on?"

"All the dogs between here and London are out barking in this cold. Now, that's real cooperation!" Tibs exclaimed.

The Colonel lifted a shaggy ear to hear the distant message, his face set with determination. "Kidnapped puppies in danger, Tibs. We've got to help!"

"I heard puppies barking at the old De Vil mansion last night," said Tibs. "You don't suppose…"

The Colonel sent a message back to London. "We'll investigate right away!" he told Tibs. They headed straight for the gloomy mansion.

The Colonel braced himself against a wall as Tibs
climbed on his shoulders to peek in a window.

"What do you see?" the Colonel barked impatiently.

"Ninety-seven, ninety-eight, ninety-nine…" Tibs
muttered. "Ninety-nine Dalmatian puppies!"

"Ninety-nine!" the Colonel exclaimed. "This operation is
bigger than we thought. We're going to need help! See what
else you can find out while I bark back to London for
reinforcements."

After the Colonel left, Tibs heard the roar of Cruella's roadster.

"The police are on our trail," Cruella told her thugs. "The puppies must be destroyed tonight!"

"They're still too little," one of the thugs protested. "The whole lot won't make three coats."

"Kill them now or I'll make a coat out of you!" Cruella
hissed. With a swirl of her great fur cape she was gone.
    "Coats!" Tibs said, horrified. "I must do something at
once!" While the thugs were watching their favorite
television show, Sergeant Tibs helped the puppies sneak out
of the room one by one.

Suddenly the thugs realized the puppies were escaping. The chase was on! Tibs and the puppies scooted through the dark and twisting halls of the mansion. They soon found themselves trapped at a dead end. The thugs raised their clubs to strike.

At that moment Pongo and Perdita crashed through the window with a spray of glass and a blast of freezing air. The angry Dalmatian parents fought off the astonished thugs as the puppies scampered to safety.

Pongo stared in disbelief at all the puppies. "Ninety-nine!" he exclaimed. "How will we ever get them all back to London?"

"We can make it if they all cooperate," Perdita declared, guiding them to a frozen stream. "If we walk over the ice, Cruella won't be able to follow our tracks."

"And if you hold on to each other, you won't fall on the ice," Pongo added as they began their perilous journey.

Along the way the Dalmatians were helped by other dogs who had heard about their escape. A black Labrador retriever arranged for the whole weary pack to ride to London in the back of a moving van that had broken down.

"Wait here in the blacksmith shop while the van is being repaired," the Labrador told the weary Dalmatians.

Through the sooty window of the blacksmith shop Perdita saw something that sent shivers skipping up the spots on her back. Cruella's roadster was parked right behind the van.

"Somehow Cruella tracked us here," Perdita cried. "How will we ever get into the van without being seen?"

Pongo thought for a moment. "If we all cooperate," he told the puppies, "we just might make it."

Cruella was surprised to see a parade of black dogs marching into the van.

"Ninety-seven, ninety-eight, ninety-nine," she counted. "But they're black as coal. They couldn't be..."

Just then little Rolly fell in the snow. The soot from the blacksmith's hearth that had covered him washed off.

"How clever! Those dogs disguised themselves with soot!" Cruella shrieked. "But I'll have their spotted hides yet!"

Cruella revved up her roadster as the van packed with Dalmatians pulled away. She rammed her car against the big van, trying to run it off the road. Instead, Cruella's roadster was sent tumbling into a ditch. The van rolled on, all the way to London.

At home that night the Dalmatians barked the joyful news of their arrival to the friends who had helped them escape. Thanks to the cooperation of the dogs of London and the countryside, and the help of a cat named Sergeant Tibs, the one hundred and one Dalmatians were safe at last.